Ella's Twinkling Wishes

By

Anne Jones

As I look up into the sky, I find the brightest star to wish upon. I recite this beautiful phrase.... *"twinkling star light up the sky, make my wish come true tonight!"*

Mom, may you continue to be my brightest star, my believer, and my hope. Continue to guide my dreams as you hear my wishes.

You are my shooting star!
I love you.

Anne Jones

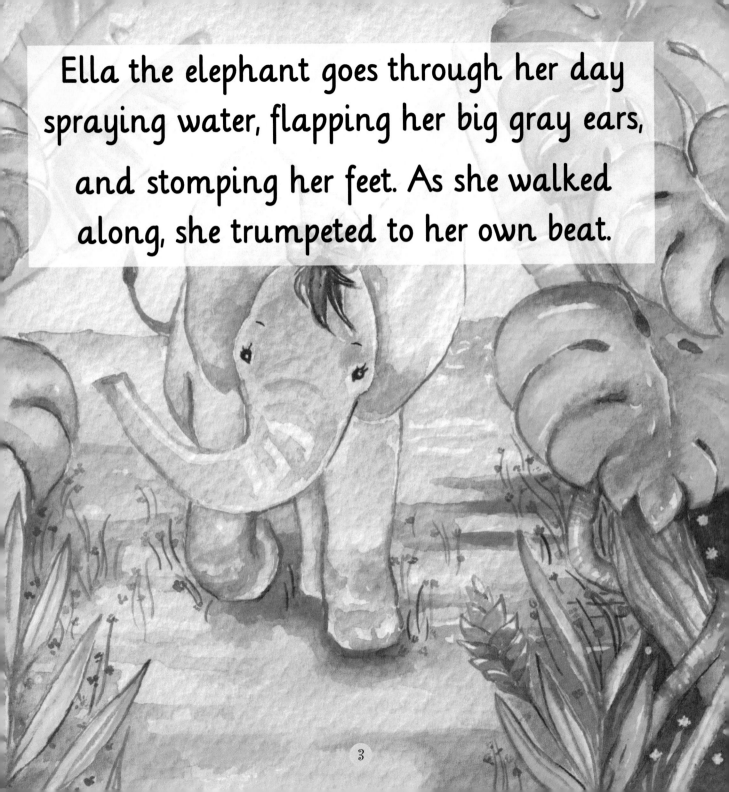

Ella the elephant goes through her day spraying water, flapping her big gray ears, and stomping her feet. As she walked along, she trumpeted to her own beat.

Each day, Ella watches the sky waiting for the night to fall. She loves the way the colors in the sky change from the endless blue sky to the dark of night.

Ella knows when the sky turns black and is filled with twinkling stars, she can search for the brightest ones to wish upon.

Ella's ears fall back as she lifts her swaying trunk to the sky and, as she gazes into the night sky, her search for the brightest star begins.

5

When Ella finally finds the perfect star, she says out loud...

Twinkling star light up the sky
Make my wish come true tonight!

Ella doesn't wish for ordinary things. She wishes for things that will fill her days with as much light and brightness as the twinkling stars in the night sky.

On Monday, Ella looked up into the sky and found the brightest star and said....

Twinkling star light up the sky
Make my wish come true tonight!

On this night, Ella wished for lasting happiness. She loved laughing, dancing, and singing, all things that make her happy. Ella dreamt of happiness that night.

The night quickly became a beautiful morning sunrise. Ella's eyes flew open with excitement. It was now Tuesday, what was she going to wish for tonight?

She walked along thinking about what feels important to her today. Before she knew it the night had fallen, and she couldn't wait tofind the brightest star. When she did, she recited....

Twinkling star light up the sky
Make my wish come true tonight!

Tonight, what was important to Ella was to wish to no longer fear things over which she had no control. Ella wanted to be liked by everyone. She felt she always had to be perfect in everything she did and last she feared being alone with no one to love her. She knew she no longer wanted to fear those things. So as Ella wished upon the star, she closed her eyes tight and when she opened them, she was surprised to see the blue sky. She had fallen asleep making her wish and it was now Wednesday.

Ella got up and began to walk. She felt happy! She was singing and dancing as she walked along. Her ears were flapping and her trunk swinging to the happiness she felt inside.

Suddenly, she stopped and froze. Ella forgot that she needed to figure out what she was going to wish for tonight. She thought and thought and, just like that, the night sky appeared, and the stars began to twinkle so bright.

It didn't take long for Ella to find the star she would wish upon. Ella looked up into the night and said ....

Twinkling star, light up the sky, make my wish come true tonight!

Ella wished for love to always fill her heart. No matter how much fear was in her heart, she would always feel an everlasting love for herself and others.

Ella tucked her trunk up onto her chest and held the feeling of being loved close to her heart and, as she did, she fell fast asleep. She knew she was lovable and would always have enough love to share with those around her.

The morning sun rose once again and, as Ella woke from a very peaceful and restful night's sleep, she felt happy, fearless, and so full of love. Ella already knew what she was going to wish for that night.
The day felt so long. She was just so excited to make her next wish. Every morning she woke up she felt inside of her all the wishes she had made come true.

Ella spent time splashing in the water, daydreaming, and napping in the hot sun.

When Ella saw the sun setting, she stood looking up into the sky with wonder. "Which star would it be tonight," she thought to herself? It was then that she spotted the star with the brightest twinkle and she knew that was the one.

Without blinking an eye, Ella looked right at that star and said....

Twinkling star light up the sky
Make my wish come true tonight!

Ella wished for lasting friendships. Friendships with which she could share her happiness, comfort each other's fears, and love one another throughout life.

19

Ella spent some time thinking about the wishes she had made. She felt excited about what Friday's night sky would provide for her to make her next wish.

The night came and went, and the day seemed to pass quickly. The night was approaching as she sat quietly watching the beautiful sun set. This wish felt so important to her and she wanted to find the perfect star, the star that could carry the weight of the wish she was about to make. Ella took a deep breath and, looking right at the star she had chosen to wish upon she whispered...

Twinkling star light up the sky
Make my wish come true tonight!

This time Ella closed her eyes, and she made her wish silently to herself. She wished to always feel safe, no matter who she was with or where she was in the world. She just wanted to hold onto her happiness, to be fierce not fearful, have a heart full of enough love to share and safety which would allow her to feel protected, no matter what.

Ella laid her head down and looked into the night sky, feeling good about the wishes she had made. But Ella did have two more wishes. She knew that rain was coming and was unsure if she would be able to see the sky's twinkling stars so she decided to ask if she could make one more BIG wish.

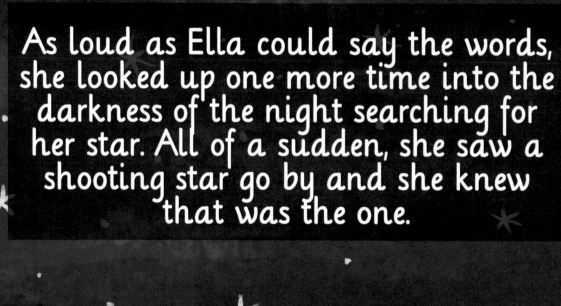

As loud as Ella could say the words, she looked up one more time into the darkness of the night searching for her star. All of a sudden, she saw a shooting star go by and she knew that was the one.

Ella's final wish before the rain was that there will always be enough twinkling stars for her to wish upon and that her wishes would continue to come true.

Anne graduated with a degree in Early Childhood Education and has been teaching young children for 27 years. Anne has always had a special interest in children's

literature and loved bringing books to life while teaching in the classroom. Anne is married with two amazing children, with whom she shared her passion for children's literature with, as they grew up.

As a child, Anne would spend time writing stories that filled her imagination. She liked creating silly characters and fun storylines that she would later read in front of a captive audience. Anne knew that one day her dream of publishing a children's book would become a reality, and she could continue to share her passion for children's literature with other young children.

When Anne was young she would sit by the window in her bedroom searching for the brightest star to wish upon. Anne would wish for the same things that Ella the Elephant would wish for when she would spot the brightest star in the sky. Ella would wish for happiness, to not fearl, for love to fill her heart, lasting friendships, to always feel safe and lastly for there always to be enough twinkling stars in the sky to wish upon.

Made in the USA
Middletown, DE
03 June 2021